This book belongs to

....

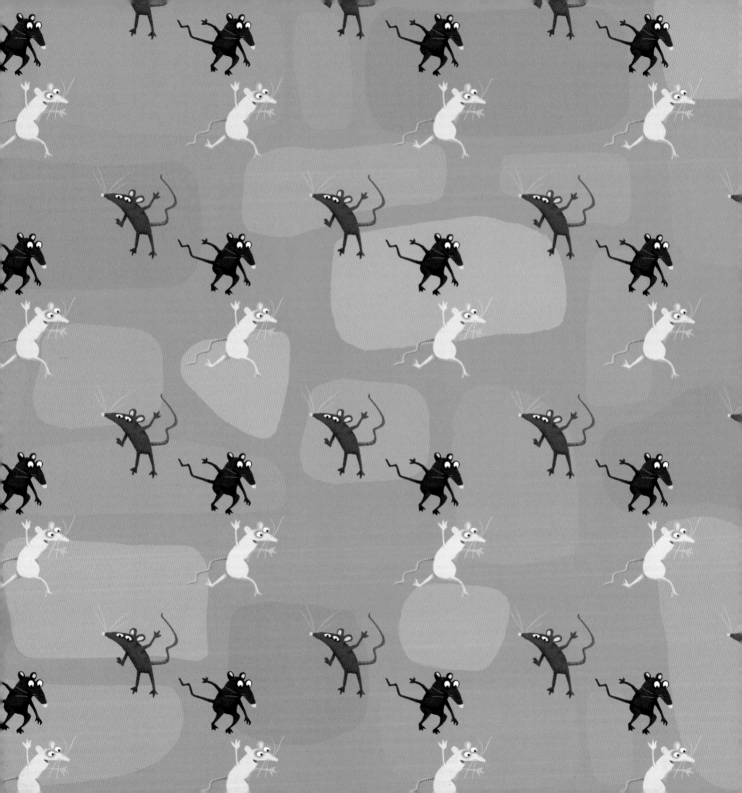

How this collection works

This collection of traditional tales offers four well-loved stories from around the world for you and your child to enjoy together: *Dick and His Cat, I Will Get You, Chicken Licken* and *Right For Me*. They are based on traditional stories that your child may already be familiar with, but have been written so that your child can read them for themselves. They are carefully levelled and in line with your child's phonics learning at school. In addition, each story is accompanied by an optional extended story text for parents to read aloud to their child, to offer the richness that the original story language provides.

How to use this book

Find a time to read with your child when they are happy to concentrate for about 5–10 minutes. Reading with your child should be a shared and enjoyable experience. Choose one or two stories for each session, so they don't get too tired.

Please read the tips on the next page of this collection, as they offer suggestions and ideas for how to get the most out of this story collection.

Enjoy sharing the stories!

Tips for reading the stories together

Step 1 – Before you begin, ask your child to read the title of the story. Talk about what the story might be about. To set the scene of the story, read the extended story text available before each story. This will provide the rich story language of the original story and will familiarise the child with the plot and the characters before they read the story for themselves. Talk about the story and what your child liked and didn"t like.

Step 2 – Now encourage your child to read the illustrated story to you. Talk about the pictures as you read. Your child will be able to read most of the words in the story, but if they struggle with a word, remind them to say the sounds in the word from left to right and then blend the sounds together to read the whole word, e.g. qu-a-ck, quack. If they come across a tricky word that they cannot sound out, simply read the word to the child, e.g. be, was.

Step 3 – After you have read the story, talk about what happened. How are all the different characters feeling at the end of the story? Encourage your child to use the story map that follows each story to retell the story to you in their own words. It's a fun way of helping them to understand the story and to learn to tell stories in their own way.

Contents

OXFORD
UNIVERSITY PRESS

Dick and His Cat

Once upon a time, there was a boy called Dick Whittington. Dick was very poor. One day, he decided to go to London to seek his fortune. So he set off down the road to London. Dick had to walk all the way. But Dick didn't mind.

"London is sure to be a wonderful place," Dick thought, "and I will be happy there."

But by the time Dick got to London, it was dark and he was cold and wet. He had no money and nowhere to stay. He sat down on the pavement and cried.

"I just want to go home!" Dick said.

But a kind man called Mr Fitzwarren helped him. Mr Fitzwarren was a rich merchant and he owned a big house in London. He said Dick could come and live in his house and work in his kitchen. Dick could hardly believe his luck!

Dick liked working for Mr Fitzwarren, except for one thing ... Mr Fitzwarren's house was overrun with rats! Dick didn't like the rats. He tried to chase them away, but they just kept coming back.

So the first time Dick was paid by Mr Fitzwarren he went to the market and spent all his money on a big cat.

Now, Dick's cat was good at catching rats. Before long, she had caught all the rats in Mr Fitzwarren's house.

Mr Fitzwarren was very pleased that Dick and his cat had got rid of all the rats. In fact, he was so pleased that he gave Dick a big sack of money.

Now that Dick had some money, he thought about going back home. But every time he thought about leaving, he heard the church bells of London ringing. The bells seemed to be telling him to stay. So he carried on working very hard in Mr Fitzwarren's kitchen.

While Dick was washing and cleaning in the kitchen, his cat was working very hard too. She worked all over the house, catching the rats, keeping them out of every room in the house.

Mr Fitzwarren saw how hard Dick and his cat worked and he paid them well. And before long they had earned sacks of gold. Now Dick could buy new clothes for himself and the best fish in all London for his cat. And they lived happily ever after.

Dick
and
His Cat

Written by Katie Adams

Illustrated by Sue Mason

Dick got his bag.

Dick met a man.

The man got Dick a job.

Dick got a cat.

The cat got a rat.

14

Dick got a bag of cash.

16

Dick got lots of jobs.

The cat got lots of rats.

Dick got lots of cash.

Dick was rich!

I am rich!
Rich! Rich!

21

Retell the story

Once upon a time...

The end.

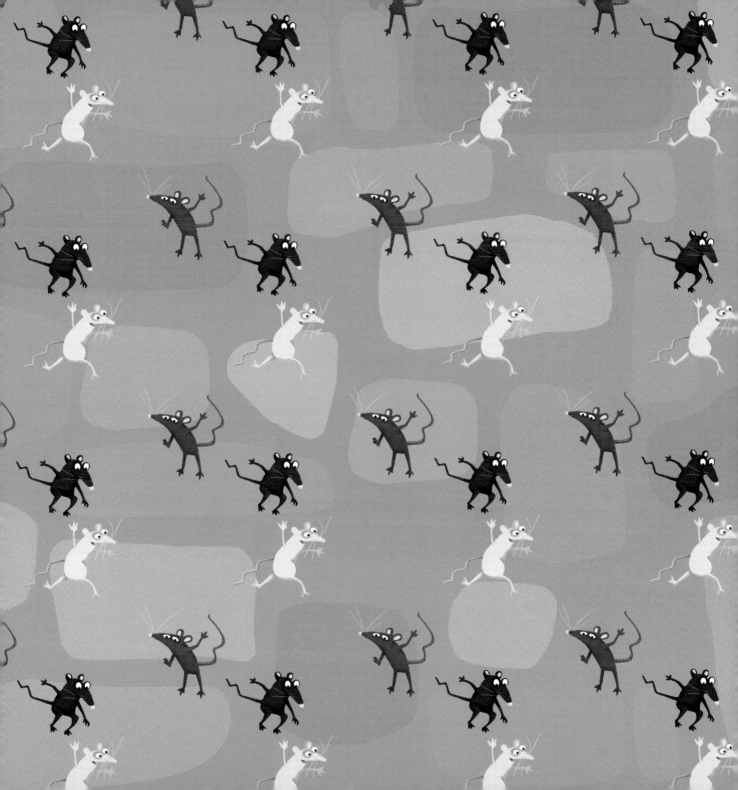

I Will Get You

Once upon a time, there were three billy goats who were brothers. One day, they went for a walk to find some grass to eat.

Soon the smallest billy goat came to a bridge. He did not know a big ugly troll lived under it. *Tip, tap, tip, tap* went the small billy goat across the bridge.

Suddenly the troll jumped up! "Who's that tip tapping across my bridge?" roared the troll.

"It's only me!" said the little goat. "Please let me cross your bridge."

"No!" said the troll. "I am going to eat you!"

The little billy goat was afraid, but he said, "I am too small to eat. Why don't you eat my brother instead? He's bigger than me!"

The troll thought and then he said, "You can go! I will eat your brother instead."

So the little billy goat ran across the bridge. *Tip, tap, tip, tap!*

Soon the middle-sized billy goat came to the bridge. He did not know a big ugly troll lived under it. *Tip, tap, tip, tap* went the middle-sized billy goat across the bridge.

Suddenly the troll jumped up! "Who's that tip tapping across my bridge?" he roared.

"It's only me!" said the middle-sized goat.

"Please let me cross your bridge."

"No!" said the troll. "I am going to eat you!"

The middle-sized billy goat was afraid, but he said, "I am too small to eat. Why don't you eat my brother instead? He's much bigger than me!"

The troll thought and then he said, "You can go! I will eat your brother instead."

So the middle-sized billy goat ran across the bridge. *Tip, tap, tip, tap!*

Soon the big billy goat came to the bridge. He did not know a big ugly troll lived under it. *Tip, tap, tip, tap* went the big billy goat across the bridge.

Suddenly the troll jumped up! "Who's that tip tapping across my bridge?" he roared.

"It's only me!" said the big billy goat. "Please let me cross your bridge."

"No!" roared the troll. "I'm going to get you!"

But the big billy goat was not afraid of the troll. He said, "No! I'm going to get **you**!"

And the big billy goat chased the troll off the bridge and down the path. So then the three billy goats settled down in the sun to eat the sweet, green grass by the bridge.

I Will Get You

Written by Alex Lane

Illustrated by Elle Daly

Tip, tap, tip, tap ...

Tip, tap, tip, tap

28

No!
Do not get me.
Get him!

Off he ran.

Tip, tap, tip, tap ...
... along the path.

No!
Do not get me.
Get him!

Off he ran.

Yum-yum!
Yes, I will get him.

Tip, tap, tip, tap ...

Quack!

35

Yum-yum!
I will get you!

37

Off he ran!

Bang!

Quack, quack, quack!

Retell the story

Once upon a time...

The end.

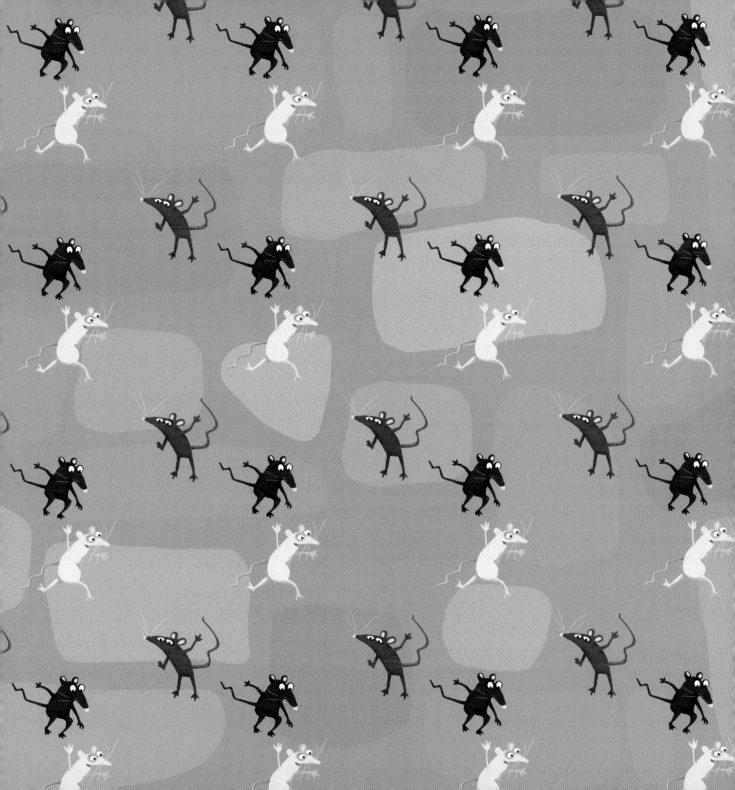

Chicken Licken Extended Story

Once upon a time, there lived a chicken called Chicken Licken. One day, she was pulling up worms under a little nut tree in the garden. Suddenly… something fell on her head!

Now, Chicken Licken was very silly.

"Ow!" she cried. "Something fell on me! It must have been the sun! Oh, dearie-me, whatever shall I do? I know! I'll go and tell Hen Len!"

And off Chicken Licken ran to the barn, as fast as her legs would carry her.

Hen Len was sitting in the barn with her chicks. "Cluck!" said Hen Len.

"Hen Len!" cried Chicken Licken. "The sun fell on me! Oh, dearie-me, whatever shall we do? Shall we go and tell Cock Lock?"

And so Chicken Licken and Hen Len ran to the farmyard, as fast as their legs would carry them.

Cock Lock was standing on the haystack. "Cock-a-doodle-doo!" said Cock Lock.

"Cock Lock!" cried Chicken Licken. "The sun fell on me! Oh, dearie-me, whatever shall we do? Shall we go and tell Duck Luck?"

And so Chicken Licken and Hen Len and Cock Lock all ran back to the garden, as fast as their legs would carry them.

Duck Luck was swimming on the duck pond.

"Quack!" said Duck Luck.

"Duck Luck!" cried Chicken Licken. "The sun fell on me! Oh, dearie-me, whatever shall we do?"

Well, Duck Luck was very surprised to hear this. "The sun, Chicken Licken?"

"Yes, Duck Luck!" cried Chicken Licken. "The sun!"

"You never stop to think, Chicken Licken," he said. "Where were you standing, when the sun fell on you?"

"Under this little nut tree in the garden," replied Chicken Licken.

"Look up, Chicken Licken," said Duck Luck. "Tell me what you can see."

"Nuts," said Chicken Licken.

"A nut fell on you, you silly chicken!" laughed Duck Luck. "Not the sun!"

"Er … a *nut*?" asked poor Chicken Licken.

"A nut!" they all laughed. "Just a nut!" So, you see, Chicken Licken really was a very silly chicken indeed!

Chicken Licken

Written by Gill Munton

Illustrated by Christine Pym

Tock!

45

Chicken Licken ran to the barn.

47

Chicken Licken and Hen Len
ran to the farmyard.

49

They all ran back to the garden.

Retell the story

Once upon a time...

The end.

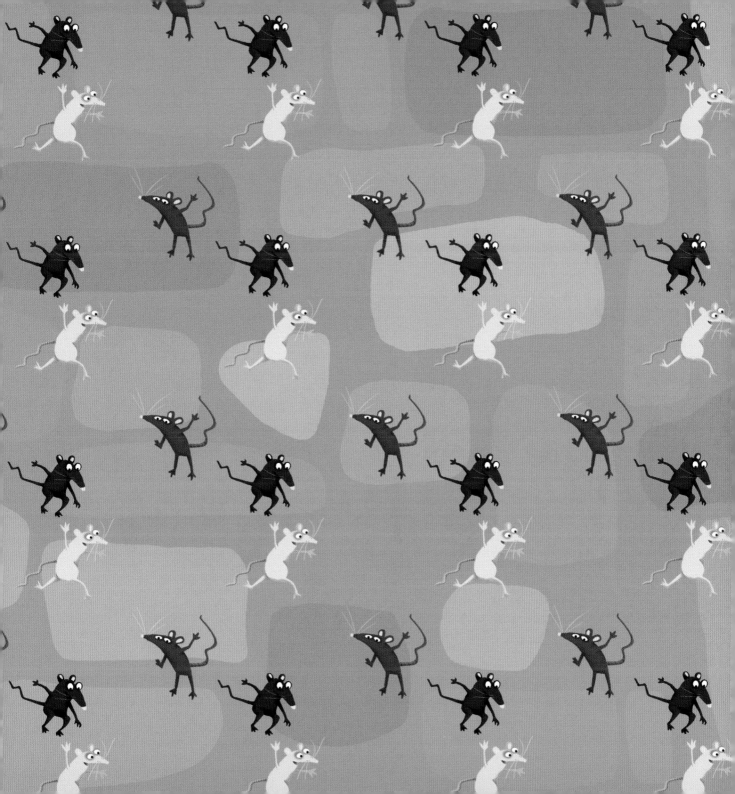

Right for Me `Extended Story`

Once upon a time, a little girl called Goldilocks was walking in the deep, dark wood. She sang as she walked, "La-la-la".

Goldilocks saw a pretty little wooden house. Now, she was a curious child, and she was also rather naughty. "What a dear little house!" she said. "I think I will go in!"

So in she went, and found herself in a cosy kitchen with a great big cooking pot. And on the table there were three bowls – all full of porridge!

Goldilocks tried the biggest bowl of porridge. "Oh!" she cried. "This porridge is too hot! I will try the middle-sized bowl!" And so she did.

"Oh!" she cried. "This porridge is too cold! I will try the smallest bowl!" And so she did.

"Ah! This porridge is just right for me!" she said. And she finished it all up.

Goldilocks went into the next room. She saw three chairs. "I think I will sit down for a while," she said. She sat on the biggest chair.

"Oh!" she cried. "This chair is too hard! I will try the middle-sized chair." And so she did.

"Oh!" she cried. "This chair is too soft! I will try the smallest chair!" And so she did.

"Ah! This chair is just right for me," she said.

Next, Goldilocks went into the bedroom. She saw three beds. "I'm tired now," she said. "I think I will lie down for a while." So she lay down on the biggest bed.

"Oh!" she cried. "This bed is too hard! I will try the middle-sized bed." And so she did.

"Oh!" she cried. "This bed is too soft! I will try the smallest bed." And so she did.

"Ah! This bed is just right for me," she said. And soon she was fast asleep.

Goldilocks didn't hear when the front door opened and someone came in! It was the three bears: Daddy Bear, Mummy Bear and Baby Bear.

"Who's been eating my porridge?" cried Baby Bear.

"Who's been sitting in my chair?" cried Baby Bear. "And who's been sleeping in my bed … Oh! she's still here!"

And naughty Goldilocks ran down the stairs, out of the little wooden house, and back home. She never went into the deep, dark wood again.

Right for Me

Written by Gill Munton

Illustrated by Ilaria Falorsi

I am in the wood!
La la la ...

I can see a log cabin!
I will go in.

This dish is
no good!

This dish is
no good!

This is the right
dish for me!

This chair is
no good!

This chair is
no good!

This is the right chair for me!

I will go into the bedroom.

This bed is
no good!

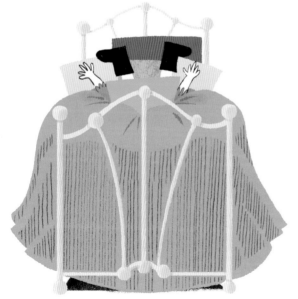

This bed is
no good!

This is the right
bed for me!

Zzzzz

Tum tee tum ...

73

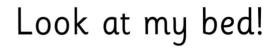

Retell the story

Once upon a time...

The end.

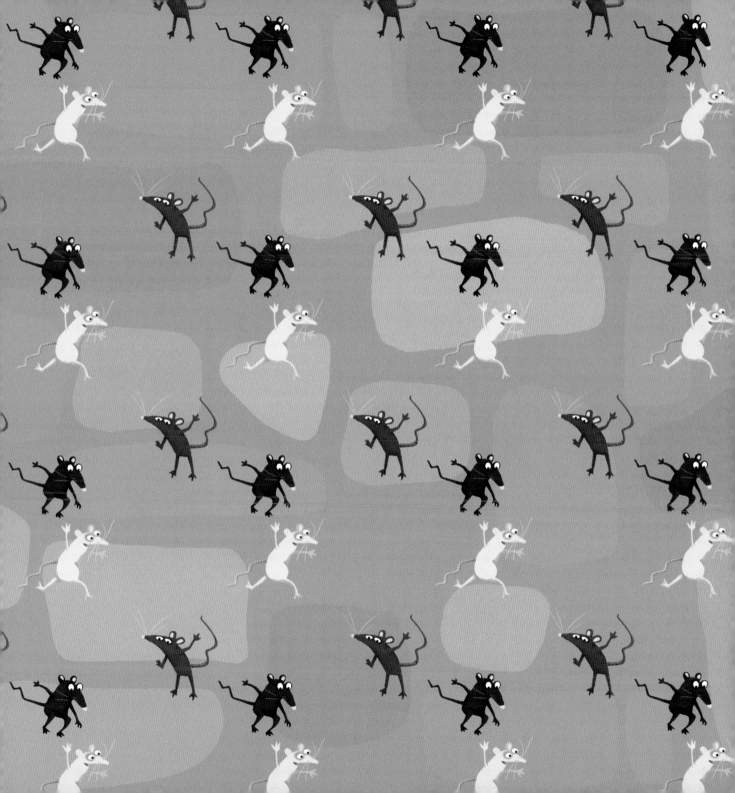

Make up a new story!

Now have a go at making up your own story like the ones in this book. You can use the ideas here or make up your own!

1 **Who is in your story?**

2 **What happens first?**

Perhaps Chicken Licken meets the troll?

Perhaps Dick and Goldilocks go off on an adventure?

3 What happens then?

Does the troll try to catch Chicken Licken?

Do Dick and Goldilocks meet a baddy?

4 How will your story end?

Will Chicken Licken give
the troll a scare instead?

Will Dick and Goldilocks
get the baddy's treasure?

OXFORD
UNIVERSITY PRESS

Great Clarendon Street, Oxford, OX2 6DP, United Kingdom

Oxford University Press is a department of the University
of Oxford. It furthers the University's objective of excellence
in research, scholarship, and education by publishing worldwide.
Oxford is a registered trade mark of Oxford University Press
in the UK and in certain other countries

British Library Cataloguing in Publication Data
Data available

ISBN: 978-0-19-276517-8

10 9 8 7 6 5 4 3 2 1

Paper used in the production of this book is a natural, recyclable
product made from wood grown in sustainable forests. The
manufacturing process conforms to the environmental
regulations of the country of origin.

Printed in China

Acknowledgements

Series Advisor: Nikki Gamble